KATIE'S KIND WORDS

By Jenna Joy

Illustrated By Sümeyye Demir

Dedicated to:

My Sister, Katie - Thank you for teaching me how affirmations can positively impact my life.

Everyday, Katie says her kind words to herself in the mirror.

"I am confident."

"I make good choices."

"I believe in myself."

"Today is a new day and I am going to have a good day!"

One day, Katie had a bad day at school.

In the morning, Katie forgot her homework.

At lunch, she spilled her juice on the floor.

At the end of the day, Katie got a bad grade on her spelling test.

When Katie got home, she went to her room and cried.

Then, she looked up at herself in the mirror and she remembered her kind words:

"I am smart."
"I try my best."
"I am enough."

Katie, then, smiled and said:

"Tomorrow is a new day and I will have a good day."

The next day at school, Katie had a reading test and she was nervous. Before the test, she quietly said some kind words to herself.

"I am focused."

"I am a good reader."

"My brain is ready for this."

Katie answered every question with confidence. At the end of the day, the teacher told her she aced the exam!

Even though yesterday was a bad day, Katie used her kind words to make sure today was a great day!

How will you use your kind words?

Here are some more kind words you can say to yourself everyday, just like Katie.

I am creative.

I am brave.

I am a good friend.

I try my best.

I have a positive attitude.

I care for others.

I can do difficult things.

There is no one quite like me!

_____'s Kind Words

Use this page to create your own kind words.

5/22

CPSIA information can be obtained
at www.ICGtesting.com
Printed in the USA
LVHW061202030522
717815LV00002B/43

9 781088 029